D0349273

This book
belongs to:

_____

Woody

Buzz

Jessie

STARRING

Slinky Dog

Bullseye

Rex

This is a Parragon book
First published in 2006

Parragon
Queen Street House
4 Queen Street
Bath, BA1 1HE, UK

ISBN 1-40547-088-7
Printed in China

Copyright © 2006 Disney Enterprises, Inc./ Pixar animation studios.

All rights reserved. No part of this publication may be reproduced, stored in a retrieval system,
or transmitted by any means, mechanical, photocopying, recording or otherwise,
without the prior permission of the copyright holder.

DISNEY · PIXAR

TOY STORY 2

𝑝

The evil Emperor Zurg appeared on the TV screen and shot Buzz
Lightyear down.

"Oh, no!" Rex moaned. He had lost his favourite Buzz Lightyear
video game... again!

The other toys tried to cheer him up – all except Woody. He was
too busy getting ready to go to Cowboy Camp with Andy.

But at the last moment, disaster struck! Woody's arm ripped whilst he and Andy were playing with Buzz.

There was not time to repair Woody, so Andy had to leave without him.

Andy's mum put Woody on the mending shelf. There, Woody met Wheezy the squeaky penguin, one of Andy's old toys. Just then Andy's mum reached up and took Wheezy from the shelf. She wanted to put him in the yard sale in the garden.

"Goodbye, Woody!" said Wheezy as he disappeared downstairs. "I'm going to rescue Wheezy!" Woody announced and he whistled for Buster, Andy's puppy. The two of them ran outside and grabbed Wheezy. But as they headed back for the house, Woody's arm tore again and he tumbled to the ground.

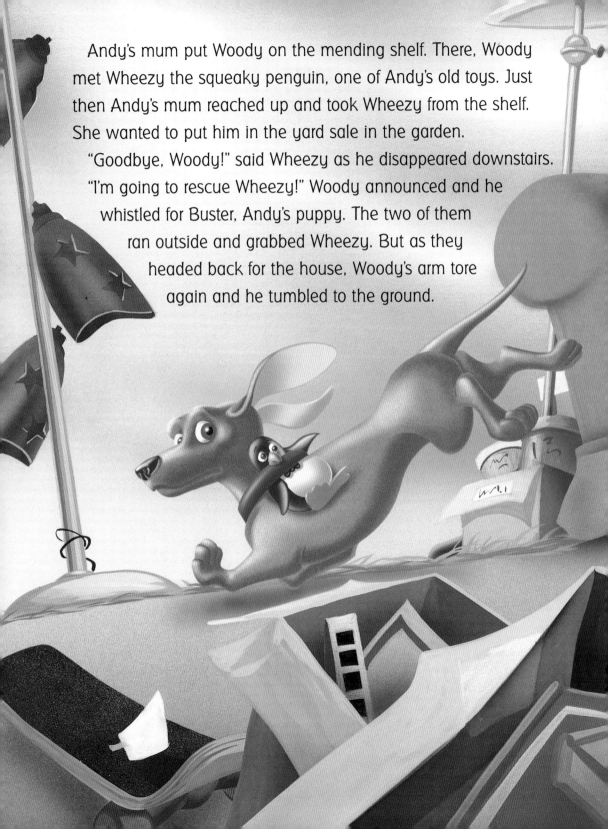

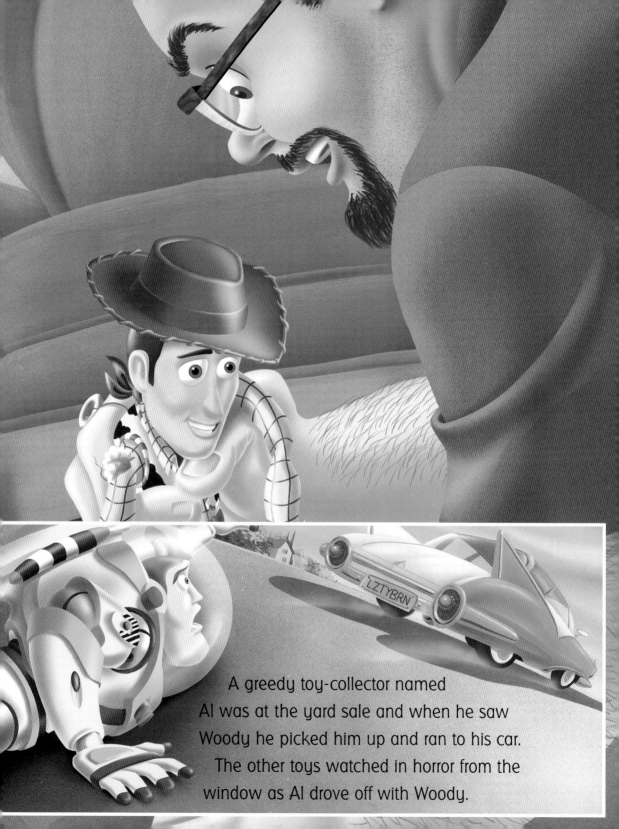

A greedy toy-collector named
Al was at the yard sale and when he saw
Woody he picked him up and ran to his car.
The other toys watched in horror from the
window as Al drove off with Woody.

Al took Woody to his apartment and locked him in. Woody looked around for a way to escape but instead he found a floppy little horse called Bullseye and a friendly cowgirl called Jessie.

"Let's show him who he really is!" said an old prospector doll in a box.

Jessie turned on the TV. Woody was amazed as he watched the show, Woody's Roundup! starring Jessie, the yodelling cowgirl, Stinky Pete the Prospector, Bullseye the horse... and Sheriff Woody!

Woody couldn't believe it. He had once been a television star, and now he was the last piece in a valuable toy collection.

"Al is selling us all to a museum in Japan," explained the Prospector.

Meanwhile, back at Andy's house, the clever toys had worked out that Al was the owner of the local toy store. That night the toys set out to rescue their friend.

Out on the rooftop, Slinky Dog held on with his paws as, one by one, Rex, Hamm and Buzz used his coils to bungee jump to the ground.

"To Al's Toy Barn… and beyond!" Buzz shouted bravely.
Then he led the way down the street. The five friends walked
on through the night. As the sun rose, they came to a busy
main road… and spotted Al's Toy Barn.

"We have to get across!" Buzz shouted.

The toys each picked up a traffic cone and dashed into the busy road. "**DROP!**" Buzz yelled and hid beneath his cone. A truck swerved to miss them, spilling its load of concrete pipes.

"**GO!**" cried Buzz.

Mr Potato Head struggled to free his shoe from a piece of bubble gum. He got away seconds before one of the pipes thundered past him.

Ignoring the honking horns and screeching brakes behind them, the toys made it safely inside the Toy Barn.

"Good job, troops!" said Buzz. "Let's split up to look around."

Not far away, Woody's arm had been repaired. He looked brand new. "I'm all ready to go home to Andy now!" said Woody.

"I belonged to a little girl once," said Jessie sadly. "She played with me every day, until she grew up. Then she gave me away. Even the greatest kids outgrow their toys. Listen, Woody, if you stay with us, you'll be remembered for ever."

"Maybe you're right," Woody said quietly. "I think I'll stay after all."

Inside the Toy Barn, Buzz looked up at an amazing display of new Buzz Lightyear toys – each one was wearing a super utility pack.

"I could use that!" thought Buzz.

WHAP! His hand was clenched by a new Buzz space ranger. And, before long, Andy's toy was overpowered and imprisoned inside a box on the shelf.

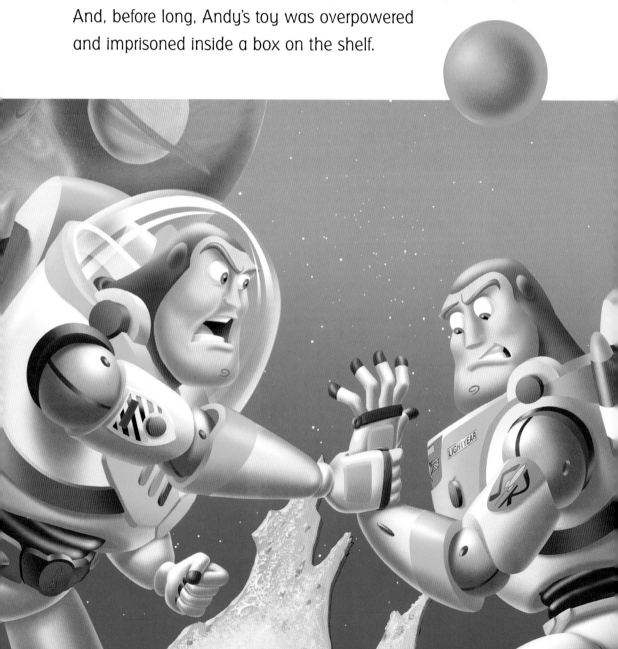

The new Buzz thought Andy's toys were on a mission to defeat the evil Emperor Zurg, so he joined Rex and the others, who were touring the store in a toy sports car. They stopped outside Al's office, and soon realised that he intended to sell Woody to a collector in Japan. They heard him discussing it over the telephone. The toys hid in Al's briefcase as he left for home.

At that very moment, the real Buzz broke free and raced after Al. But Buzz was being followed... by the evil Emperor Zurg!

Once inside Al's apartment, the toys escaped from his briefcase. New Buzz rushed up to Bullseye. "We're here. Woody!" he yelled.

Andy's toys looked at the New Buzz suspiciously. Then Andy's real Buzz appeared. The toys were confused!

"There's no time to explain," Andy's Buzz said to everyone. "Come on, Woody! Let's go!" But to his amazement, Woody refused.

"Yeah!" Woody said sadly. "When I'm worn out, Andy will just throw me away." He turned around and switched on the TV.

Woody watched a small smiling boy on the TV screen. It made him realise just how much he missed Andy. "Hey, Buzz! Wait!" he shouted. But the Prospector blocked the way.

Buzz turned to help his friend but just then Al came into the room. He scooped his valuable toys into a suitcase and took them to the airport!

"We have to get Woody," Buzz shouted. But as they headed for the lift on Al's floor, they heard an evil laugh.

"It's Zurg!" gasped Rex.

Bravely Buzz and the New Buzz fought off the attack. Rex closed his eyes in panic. Then **THWACK**! His tail knocked Zurg off the roof. "I won! I defeated Zurg!" Rex shouted excitedly.

Andy's toys said goodbye to the New Buzz and raced through the hall after Woody.

Luckily, Mr Potato Head spotted a pizza truck nearby and the toys jumped in. And so, with Buzz at the steering wheel, Slinky on the pedals, Rex as navigator, and Hamm and Mr Potato Head working the levers, they zigzagged their way to the airport. There, the toys ran inside, desperately looking for Al.

They found him – he was still at the check-in desk. As Al's suitcase thumped onto the conveyor belt, the toys jumped on beside it.

Thousands of boxes, bags and suitcases swept past them. But Buzz kept his eyes on Al's green suitcase.

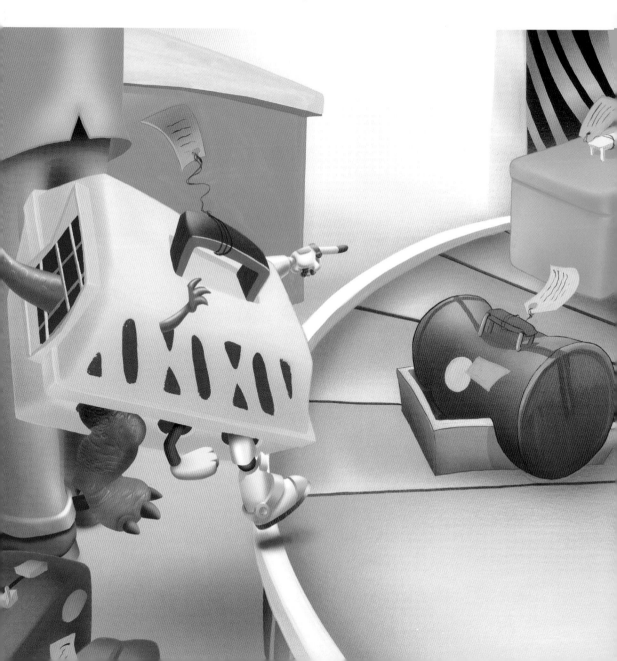

"Woody, are you in there?" he called, and he opened the catch.

POW! The prospector came out fighting. Buzz fought back and quickly packed him in a backpack.

Woody and Bullseye had managed to get out of Al's suitcase but Jessie was still trapped inside.

"I'm NOT letting Jessie down!" Woody thought. "She deserves another chance to play with a kid who loves her."

Woody, Buzz and Bullseye galloped after Jessie towards the plane.

Woody dived into a golf bag, as it was loaded on the plane. Then he searched the bags, until he found Jessie.

"Oh, Woody, I knew you'd come!" she cried.

"We're not out of here yet!" said Woody grimly. "And we haven't much time left!"

They felt the plane begin to move towards the runway.
Woody tried to help Jessie down, but his weak arm gave way...
"**HELP!**" she cried, as she fell towards the wheel.

Thinking quickly, Woody used his string as a lasso and pulled Jessie up safely.

At the same moment, Bullseye and Buzz galloped towards them. "Jump! Woody! Jump!" called Buzz.

So, holding Jessie tightly, Woody dropped onto Bullseye's back.

Later that day, Andy and his mum arrived back. Andy was delighted to be home. And he was even more pleased to see Bullseye and Jessie with the other toys on his bed! He started to play with them at once.

The toys all smiled. They were safe at last – back in Andy's room!